Percy
and the Badger

Written and illustrated by
Nick Butterworth

Collins

Percy the Park Keeper
was in the park.
He saw his friend
the badger.
Percy said, "Hello.
You *do* look muddy!"

4

Percy had an idea.
He got out his old tin bath.
Percy said, "Come and
have a bath."
The badger said, "Oh, no!"
He didn't want a bath.

Percy got out his jug and
his bath cap.
He said, "Where's that badger?"

The badger had gone.
Percy looked and looked…
…but he couldn't find
the badger at all.

Then Percy had another idea.
He said, "The badger doesn't want
a bath, but *I* do."
He got into the bath!

Percy said, "Where *is* that badger?"

CRACK! What was that?
The badger fell out of a tree
into the bath!
SPLASH!

Percy laughed. "Well, well!
You *are* having a bath, after all!"

A storyboard

:paw: Ideas for guided reading :paw:

Learning objectives: Using a variety of cues when reading; reading independently, matching spoken and written words; reading and spelling CVC words; retelling a story in own words.

Curriculum links: Geography: our local area; Citizenship: animals and us

High frequency words: saw, his, do, had, an, got, out, want, where, that, laugh, after

Interest words: badger, bath, muddy, crack, splash

Word count: 132

Resources: small whiteboards and pens

Getting started

- Ask the children questions about the front cover illustration. Why is Percy wearing a hat? Discuss what the story might be about. Read the title together.

- Walk through the book looking at the pictures and stop at p9. What do the children think will happen? Why doesn't the badger want a bath?

- Ask them to find CVC words (p6 *got, jug, bath, cap*) and sound them out aloud. Point out that *th* makes one sound.

Reading and responding

- Ask the children to read aloud and independently until p9. Observe, prompt and praise children for matching spoken and written words, and for using different cues to read unfamiliar words (e.g. picture cues for *badger*, sounding out for *tin*).

- At p9, check the children's predictions on what will happen next. Then read on to p13 and find out if they're right.

- Discuss how Percy and the badger feel at the end of the story.

- When you've read the story ask the children to look at the storyboard on pp14-15. Ask them to describe what is happening in each of the pictures.